THIS WALKER BOOK BELONGS TO:

_____

_____

_____

_____

Ling

Maddy

Alphonse

Harry

Claudia

Vikram

Georgia

Archie

**For Edward, Clare,
Alexander and Anna**

First published 1999 by Walker Books Ltd
87 Vauxhall Walk, London SE11 5HJ

This edition published 2000

2 4 6 8 10 9 7 5 3

© 1999 Zita Newcome

This book has been typeset in AT Arta Medium.

Printed in China

British Library Cataloguing in Publication Data
A catalogue record for this book is
available from the British Library.

ISBN 0-7445-7787-X

Toddlerobics
Animal Fun

Zita Newcome

WALKER BOOKS
AND SUBSIDIARIES
LONDON · BOSTON · SYDNEY

Give yourself a jiggle, come join in –

Animal Fun is about to begin!

Waddle like a penguin from side to side,

Flip your fins – imagine you're a fish!

back straight, arms down, feet out wide.

Swim through the sea with a splish, splash, splish!

Scuttle
like a crab
on your feet
and hands.

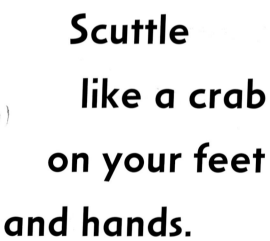

Thisaway,
  thataway,
    across
      the sands.

Hands can be starfish –

stretch fingers wide.

Now floating jellyfish,

swirling in the tide.

Quack
like a duck
and
bend down low.

Move
your elbows
to and fro.

Squat
like a frog,
flick your
tongue in the sky.

Jump
right up and
catch that fly!

Roar!
You're a lion!

Snap!
You're a croc!

Be a kangaroo!
Go hop, hop, hop!

Swing your arms like a monkey in a tree.

Whoop and scratch and jump with glee!

Stomp like an elephant,

Circle round the room with a

lift that trunk.

thump, thump, thump!

Put hands together, make a hissing snake.

Gallop like a horse, give your mane a shake!

Flutter
your
wings –
be a
butterfly.

Swoop
down low,
then
soar up
high.

Lie on
your tummy,

wriggle like
a worm.

Roll and
writhe,

twist and
squirm.

Take deep
breaths
as you lie
on the ground.

Sssshh!
Curl up
and don't
make a sound.

That was GREAT!

Let's all take a bow.

Toddlerobics is fun

when you know how!

Ling

Maddy

Alphonse

Harry

Claudia

Vikram

Georgia

Archie

Toddlerobics: Animal Fun

ZITA NEWCOME says, "Working regularly with young children, you get a very good picture of what they enjoy and respond to. I've noticed that children *love* any rhyme that enables them to move like animals or 'speak' like them. It seems to really let loose their imaginations and high spirits. So I thought I'd make up a whole book of animal movements and noises with bouncy rhymes and pictures. The key for whoever is actually reading the book is to try the actions too. Then everyone gets a good bit of exercise, and the child gets the happy opportunity of seeing their parent or nursery teacher waddling like a duck!"

Zita Newcome's first children's book arose from a greetings card she illustrated featuring four hippos. Her husband, Robert, wrote a story about the hippos and a series of three books resulted. Since then Zita has produced many books for Walker, including *Toddlerobics*, which won the Oppenheim Toy Portfolio Book Award and has sold over 65,000 copies to date. Zita has two children and lives in Maidenhead.

More toddler fun

ISBN 0-7445-5229-X (pb)

ISBN 0-7445-7752-7 (pb)

ISBN 0-7445-7797-7 (pb)